HAMMER and nails

Written by Josh Bledsoe
Illustrated by Jessica Warrick

For Allie and Wes, who
unknowingly pushed me to
write. This is our story.
Love, Dad. –JB

To Dad, my best project partner,
who made the garage into my
favorite room. –JW

Printed in China.

ISBN:
Hardcover 9781936261369
ePDF 9781936261482
EPUB 9781936261833
KF8 9781936261840

Cataloging-in-Publication details are available
from the Library of Congress.

Editor: Shari Dash Greenspan
Graphic Design: The Virtual Paintbrush

This book is typeset in Jingle Condensed. Cover fonts are
Anderson Stingray designed by Steve Zodiac Ferrera, and
Fabulous 50s. The art was created with a mixture of
watercolor and digital paint.

Flashlight Press • 527 Empire Blvd. • Brooklyn, NY 11225
www.FlashlightPress.com

Distributed by IPG

Darcy crumpled up her playdate plans and plopped onto her bed.

Her best friend was sick, and now Darcy's entire day was ruined.

Daddy overheard the grumbling and knocked on Darcy's door.

Daddy had a list of his own. "Hey, Squirt. I've got an idea. What about having a Darcy-Daddy Day?"

Darcy scowled. "What does that mean?"

"Well, we'd do one thing from my list and then one thing from your list until everything on both lists gets done."

“Oh, Daddy. I don’t know if you’ll
like doing the things on my — ”

“Whoa, whoa, whoa!” Daddy interrupted.
“Give me a chance!
Just uncrumple your list
and come downstairs.
It’s coffee time. We sip.
We read. We relax.”

“Can it be chocolate milk
time for me?”

“Sure thing,” Daddy answered.

COMICS

Next it was Darcy's turn. "The first thing on my list was Dress Up, but — "

"FANTASTIC!" Daddy said. "These PJs are so unfashionable. Were you thinking fancy or super fancy?"

Darcy grinned. "Super fancy, Daddy."

"Excellent."
Daddy disappeared.

A few minutes later, Darcy was digging for a red slipper when she heard, "Ta-da! Is this fancy enough?"

Darcy giggled. “How did you fit into my tutu, Daddy?”

Daddy laughed. “It wasn’t easy! Now, Princess, I hope you don’t mind getting your gown dirty. Meet me on the porch in five minutes.”

Daddy called it Her Majesty's Mowing Service, hoping to bring a little glamour to grass cutting.

After several sharp turns and zigzags, Darcy was amazed at what they'd created.

“Daddy, is that my name in the grass?!”

“Indeed, milady!
This is your castle!”

Darcy beamed.
"This is fun! My pick now!
We need to freshen up.
It's time for Hair Salon."

Daddy agreed.
"I'm definitely un-fresh
and my hair is a wreck!"

After
curling
and
spraying
and
combing
and
brushing,

Daddy had a daring new style and Darcy had an even more dazzling 'do.

"We look fabulous," announced Darcy.

"Totally fabulous," answered Daddy. "And now I'm choosing…

…laundry! It's time
for battle, Princess.
Take no prisoners –

and leave no sock unmatched!"

To celebrate their victory,
Darcy called for dancing in the kingdom.

Then Daddy called
for ice packs and
a royal rest.

After a picnic lunch
and a quick cleanup,
Daddy fetched his
tool belt from the garage.
"Now Darcy, I don't
know if you'll like — "

"Whoa, whoa, whoa!"
Darcy interrupted.
"Give me
a chance!"

“Fair enough. We need to fix the fence around your castle. Take this hammer and follow me. I’ll tap the nails into the loose boards and you’ll pound them in.”

Darcy’s eyes got big. This was harder than riding the mower or folding some socks. This was real work! What if she missed the nail? Smashed the fence? Smooshed her thumb?

Daddy adjusted his headband and smiled. “Princess, sometimes things you’ve never done end up being fun. Try it.”

Darcy nodded.

After a few practice taps, Darcy got the hang of it and became the best nail-pounding princess in the kingdom.

"Castle secure," she announced when the last board was fixed.

Darcy dusted off her hands and noticed her nails. "Okay, Daddy. The last thing on my list is the best. It's time for…

…**manicures!**”

This time, Daddy’s eyes got big.
Nail polish seemed so…
permanent. Not like
a funny outfit or
a wacky hair-do.

Darcy adjusted
her tiara and smiled.
“Daddy, sometimes things
you’ve never done end up
being fun! Try it!”

Daddy nodded.

After trimming and filing, it was time for polish. Darcy chose Lime-a-Bean Green and Daddy chose Lumberjack Black. After a few smudges, Daddy got the hang of it and became the best nail-painting daddy in the kingdom.

As their nails dried,
Darcy looked at her
silly daddy with his
crooked headband and
grass-stained tutu.

Then she looked at her
own grass-stained gown
and purse full of tools.
"Daddy, thank you for
my Darcy-Daddy Day."

"My pleasure, Princess.
You were great with
that hammer."

“And Daddy — you were great with these nails.”